Thank you, Mr. Falker

PATRICIA POLACCO

Thank you, Mr. Falker

SCHOLASTIC INC.
New York Toronto London Auckland Sydney
Mexico City New Delhi Hong Kong

ISBN 0-439-09836-X

Published by Scholastic Inc., 555 Broadway, New York, NY 10012, by arrangement with Philomel Books a division of Penguin Putnam Inc.

35 34 33 16/0

Printed in the U.S.A. 40

First Scholastic printing, September 1999

Patricia Lee Gauch, Editor.
Book designed by Donna Mark. Text set in Garth Graphic.

Now, almost every day after school, she met with Mr. Falker and Miss Plessy, a reading teacher. They did a lot of things she didn't even understand! At first she made circles in sand, and then big sponge circles on the blackboard, going from left to right, left to right.

Another day they flicked letters on a screen, and Trisha shouted them out loud. Still other days she worked with wooden blocks and built words. Letters, letters, letters. Words, words, words. Always sounding them out. And that felt good.

But, though she'd read words, she hadn't read a whole sentence. And deep down she still felt dumb.

And then one spring day—had it been three months or four months since they had started?—Mr. Falker put a book in front of her. She'd never seen it before. He picked a paragraph in the middle of a page and pointed at it.

Almost as if it were magic, or as if light poured into her brain, the words and sentences started to take shape on the page as they never had before. "She...marched...them...off...to..." Slowly, she read a sentence. Then another, and another. And finally she'd read a paragraph. And she understood the whole thing.

She didn't notice that Mr. Falker and Miss Plessy had tears in their eyes.

But Mr. Falker caught her arm and sank to his knees in front of her. "You poor baby," he said. "You think you're dumb, don't you? How awful for you to be so lonely and afraid."

She sobbed.

"But, little one, don't you understand, you don't see letters or numbers the way other people do. And you've gotten through school all this time, and fooled many, many good teachers!" He smiled at her. "That took cunning, and smartness, and such, such bravery."

Then he stood up and finished washing the board. "We're going to change all that, girl. You're going to read—I promise you that."

Trisha was sure Mr. Falker believed that she could read. She had learned to memorize what the kid next to her was reading. Or she would wait for Mr. Falker to help her with a sentence, then she'd say the same thing that he did. "Good," he would say.

Then, one day, Mr. Falker asked her to stay after school and help wash the blackboards. He put on music and brought out little sandwiches as they worked and talked.

All at once he said, "Let's play a game! I'll shout out letters. You write them on the board with the wet sponge as quickly as you can."

"A," he shouted. She wiped a watery A.

"Eight," he shouted. She made a watery 8.

"Fourteen . . . Three . . . D . . . M . . . Q," he shouted out. He shouted out many, many letters and numbers. Then he walked up behind her, and together they looked at the board.

It was a watery mess. Trisha knew that none of the letters or numbers looked like they should. She threw the sponge down and tried to run.

But one day at recess, Eric followed her to her secret hiding place. "Have you become a mole?" he laughed. And he pulled her out into the hall, and danced around her. "Dumbbell, dumbbell, magotty old dumbbell!"

Trisha buried her head in her arms and curled up in a ball. Suddenly, she heard footsteps. It was Mr. Falker.

He marched Eric down to the office. When he came back, he found Trisha. "I don't think you'll have to worry about that boy again," he said softly.

"What was he teasing you about, little one?"

"I don't know." Trisha shrugged.

But the nicer Mr. Falker was to Trisha, the worse Eric treated her. He got all the other kids to wait for her on the playground, or in the cafeteria, or even in the bathroom, and to jump out and call her "Stupid!" or "Ugly!"

And Trisha began to believe them.

She discovered that if she asked to go to the bathroom just before recess, she could hide under the inside stairwell during the free time, and not have to go outside at all. In that dark place she felt completely safe.

In first grade, Trisha sat in a circle with the other kids. They were all holding *Our Neighborhood*, their first reader, sounding out letters and words. They said, "Beh, beh . . . oy, boy, and luh, luh . . . ook, look." The teacher smiled at them when they put all the sounds together and got a word right.

But when Trisha looked at a page, all she saw were wiggling shapes, and when she tried to sound out words, the other kids laughed at her.

"Trisha, what are you looking at in that book?" they'd say.

"I'm reading!" she'd say back to them.

But her teacher would move on to the next person. Always when it was her turn to read, her teacher had to help her with every single word. And while the other kids moved up into the second reader and third reader, she stayed alone in *Our Neighborhood*.

Trisha began to feel "different." She began to feel dumb.

LOOK, LOOK.

Trisha, the littlest girl in the family, grew up loving books. Her schoolteacher mother read to her every night. Her redheaded brother brought his books home from school and shared them. And whenever she visited the family farm, her grandfather or grandmother read to her by the stone fireplace.

When she turned five and went to kindergarten, most of all she hoped to read. Each day she saw the kids in the first grade across the hall reading, and before the year was over, some of the kids in her own class began to read. Not Trisha.

Still, she loved being at school because she could draw. The other kids would crowd around her and watch her do her magic with the crayons.

"In first grade, you'll learn to read," her brother said.

The grandpa held the jar of honey so that all the family could see, then dipped a ladle into it and drizzled honey on the cover of a small book.

The little girl had just turned five.

"Stand up, little one," he cooed. "I did this for your mother, your uncles, your older brother, and now you!"

Then he handed the book to her. "Taste!"

She dipped her finger into the honey and put it into her mouth.

"What is that taste?" the grandma asked.

The little girl answered, "Sweet!"

Then all of the family said in a single voice, "Yes, and so is knowledge, but knowledge is like the bee that made that sweet honey, you have to chase it through the pages of a book!"

The little girl knew that the promise to read was at last hers. Soon she was going to learn to read.

To George Felker, the real Mr. Falker.
You will forever be my hero.

That night, Trisha ran home without stopping to catch her breath. She bounded up the front steps, threw open her front door, and ran through the dining room to the kitchen. She climbed up on the cupboard and grabbed a jar of honey.

Then she went into the living room and found the book on a shelf, the very book that her grandpa had shown her so many years ago. She spooned honey on the cover and tasted the sweetness, and said to herself, "The honey is sweet, and so is knowledge, but knowledge is like the bee who made the honey, it has to be chased through the pages of a book!"

Then she held the book, honey and all, close to her chest. She could feel tears roll down her cheeks, but they weren't tears of sadness—she was happy, so very happy.

The rest of the year became an odyssey of discovery and adventure for the little girl. She learned to love school. I know because that little girl was me, Patricia Polacco.

I saw Mr. Falker again some thirty years later at a wedding. I walked up to him and introduced myself. At first he had difficulty placing me. Then I told him who I was, and how he had changed my life so many years ago.

He hugged me and asked me what I did for a living. "Why, Mr. Falker," I answered. "I make books for children.... Thank you, Mr. Falker. Thank you."

Great Titles *from* C&T PUBLISHING

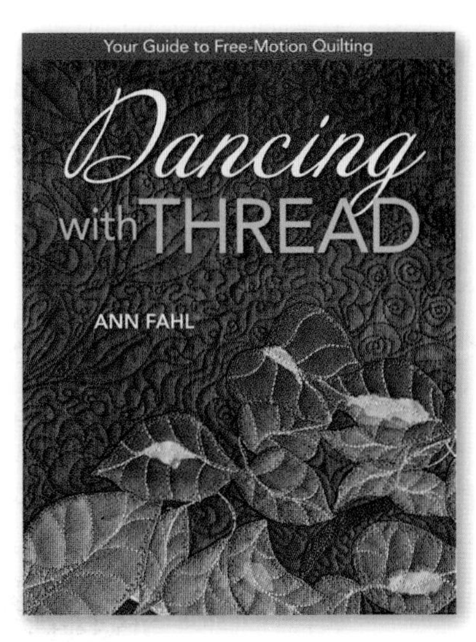

Available at your local retailer or **www.ctpub.com** *or* **800-284-1114**

For a list of other fine books from C&T Publishing, visit our website to view our catalog online

C&T PUBLISHING, INC.

P.O. Box 1456
Lafayette, CA 94549
800-284-1114

Email: ctinfo@ctpub.com
Website: www.ctpub.com

C&T Publishing's professional photography services are now available to the public. Visit us at www.ctmediaservices.com.

Tips and Techniques can be found at www.ctpub.com > Consumer Resources > Quiltmaking Basics: Tips & Techniques for Quiltmaking & More

For quilting supplies:

COTTON PATCH

1025 Brown Ave.
Lafayette, CA 94549
Store: 925-284-1177
Mail order: 925-283-7883

Email: CottonPa@aol.com
Website: www.quiltusa.com

Note: Fabrics used in the quilts shown may not be currently available, as fabric manufacturers keep most fabrics in print for only a short time.

About the Author

Photo by Karen Bowers/Shoot for the Moon

Judi Warren Blaydon grew up observing that almost the only days her grandmother's dining room table was not covered by a quilt-in-progress were Thanksgiving and Christmas. She also learned that fabric was a more valuable commodity than a fur coat and that heirloom family quilts were to be treated as treasures. Judi began as a painter, making large acrylic paintings about quilts. It was that same grandmother who said, "If you love them so much, why don't you make a real one?"

With a background in art education, Judi began teaching The Great American Quilt class in the School of Design Adult Program at the Toledo Museum of Art in Ohio in 1976. She currently lectures, judges, and teaches for conferences and guilds in the United States, Switzerland, and Japan.

Judi's Master of Fine Arts degree was perhaps one of the earliest in which the major media was quilts. Her work has been shown at the New England Quilt Museum, at Quilt National and Crafts National exhibitions, and represented in public and private collections in the United States, Australia, and Japan. Her quilts are in 28 books, including Nihon Vogue's *88 Leaders in the Quilt World Today* and Robert Shaw's *The Art Quilt.* Her quilt *The Mountain and the Magic: Night Lights* is in the permanent collection of the Museum of the American Quilter's Society in Paducah, Kentucky.

Judi and her husband, Frank, live in Milford, Michigan, where Judi makes her quilts and where her flower garden is primarily a salad bar enjoyed by deer and rabbits. Judi will be happy to schedule a Collage+Cloth=Quilt workshop for your group. Contact her at blay555@yahoo.com for information about her lectures and workshops.